For Eugene,
who has just the right number of toys

First U.S. edition 2015

Library of Congress Catalog Card Number 2014949928
ISBN 978-0-7636-7861-6

TWP 20 19 18 17 16 15
10 9 8 7 6 5 4 3 2 1

Printed in Johor Bahru, Malaysia

This book was typeset in Alghera.
The illustrations were done ink and watercolor and rendered digitally.

Candlewick Press
99 Dover Street
Somerville, Massachusetts 02144

visit us at www.candlewick.com

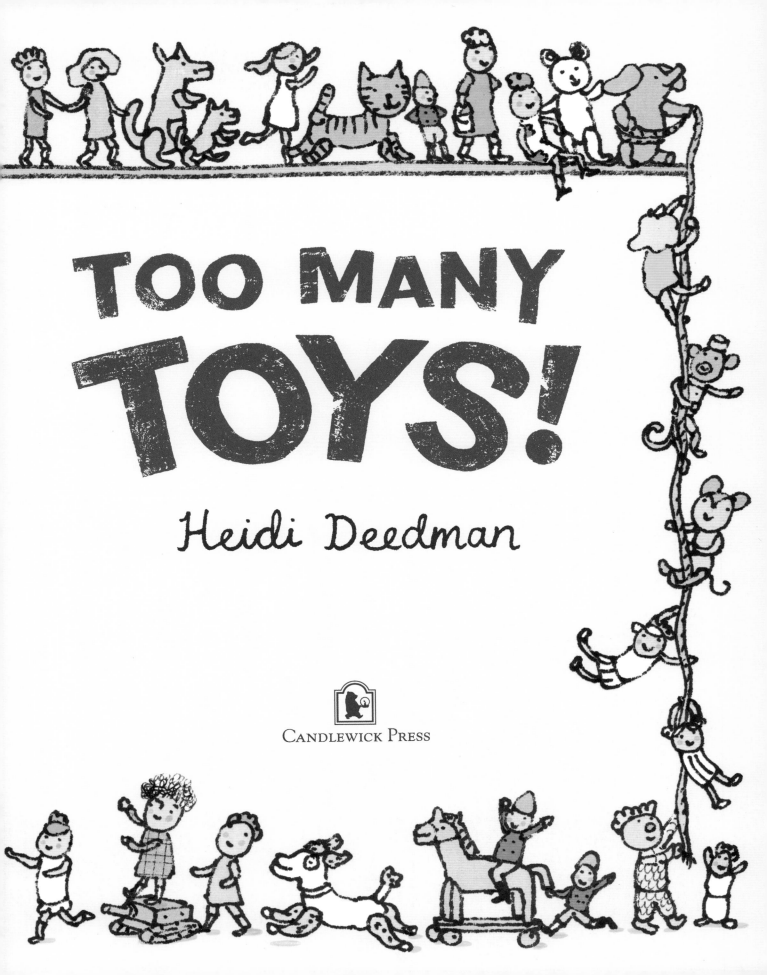

TOO MANY TOYS!

Heidi Deedman

CANDLEWICK PRESS

When Lulu was a baby, she was given
a very special one-and-only toy —

a lovely fluffy teddy bear.

Lulu named him Jupiter,

and she loved him very, very much.

As Lulu grew, she was given
more toys to play with.

And more toys . . .

and MORE toys.

But no matter how
many toys she got,
Jupiter was always
her favorite.

When Lulu was five years old,
she had a birthday party.
There were balloons and cake
and lots of games.

There were also
LOTS of presents, which meant . . .

LOTS MORE TOYS!

It was getting harder and harder
to find room for all of Lulu's toys.

Her shelves
were full.

Her toy box
wouldn't close.

Breakfast time was messy.

TV time
was noisy.

Playtime was
rowdy.

Bath time was splishy-splashy.

And then . . .

IT WAS CHRISTMAS.

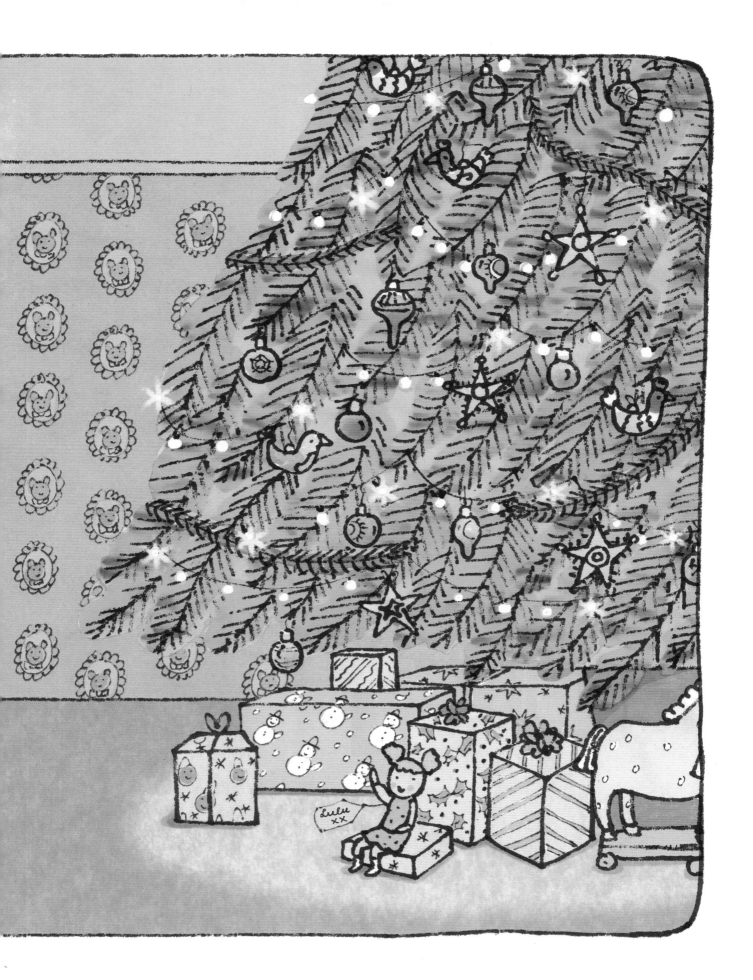

Lulu just had TOO MANY TOYS!

"What are we going
to do, Jupiter?"
asked Lulu. "I can't
play with everybody!"

She thought
hard.

She made up
her mind.

Lulu had a plan. . . .

She put all her toys together
in a GREAT BIG
ENORMOUS pile.

(Have you ever seen so many toys?)

Now she was ready for . . .

All her friends came,
from far and wide.

And Lulu gave away . . .

a big soft dog,

a wagon with a dog,
a pig, and a
teddy girl
in it,

a walking,
talking robot,

a doll that said
"Mama,"

two more dolls,

even more dolls,

three soldiers
(and their horse),

a musical monkey,

a family of dogs,

a lion with a curly
mane,

her dollhouse and all
its furniture,

a sort of gonk,

a striped cat,

a box of cars,

a big kite,

and lots more
until all the toys
were gone.

W<small>ait</small>—

ALL the toys?

Did Lulu keep
anything at all?

Of course she did.

She kept Jupiter,
    her one-and-only.
He was *much* too special
    to give away.

"Jupiter, you are all I need,"
said Lulu.

Still ...

there might be a tiny bit of space
for just a few more toys
next Christmas.